W9-BNZ-852

LaRue Across America

POSTCARDS FROM THE VACATION

written & illustrated by

MARK TEAGUE

SCHOLASTIC INC.
NEW YORK   TORONTO   LONDON   AUCKLAND   SYDNEY   NEW DELHI   HONG KONG

The Snort City R

July 10

for Laura

Designed by David Saylor and Kathleen Westray.

No part of this publication may be reproduced in whole or in part, or stored in a retrieval system, or transmitted in any form or by any means, electronic, mechanical, photocopying, recording, or otherwise, without written permission of the publisher. For information regarding permission, write to Scholastic Inc., 557 Broadway, New York, NY 10012.

Copyright © 2011 by Mark Teague.
All rights reserved. Published by Scholastic Inc.
Printed in the U.S.A.

ISBN-13: 978-0-545-34236-0
ISBN-10: 0-545-34236-8

SCHOLASTIC and associated logos are trademarks
and/or registered trademarks of Scholastic Inc.

3 4 5 6 7 8 9 10   08   20 19 18 17 16 15 14 13 12

HEAT WAVE HARMS HIBBINS!

LARUE CANCELS CRUISE

his week's record-setting heat wave laimed another victim yesterday s Leona Hibbins of Second Avenue ainted and had to be rushed to the hospital. Though Hibbins appears unharmed, the tragedy has left her two cats stranded.

Fortunately neighbor Gertrude LaRue has offered to help by taking the cats with her on a spur-of-the-moment vacation. "My dog, Ike, and I had been planning a cruise," LaRue explained. "But the ship doesn't allow cats, so I have decided to go on a driving tour instead. Really, I couldn't be happier with the change in plans. Cruises always make me seasick, and Ike just adores the cats."

Mrs. Hibbins, contacted in the hospital, described the offer as "generous," though she did express some misgivings. "My cats don't always get along with that dog."

HIBBINS RESCUED

July 10

Dear Mrs. Hibbins,

Somehow Mrs. LaRue has convinced herself that a cross-country drive—with your cats!—is a good idea. Aside from the fact that she and I are <u>supposed</u> to be departing soon on a cruise to Mexico, there is the important issue of safety to be considered. You know that she has never been a skillful driver. What if the car breaks down in some hideous wasteland? I have tried to reason with her, but without success. Perhaps <u>you</u> could persuade her to abandon this ridiculous scheme.

Your Concerned Neighbor,
Ike

July 11, Smash and Splash Water World,
WOMPASCONSETT, CONNECTICUT

Dear Mrs. Hibbins,

We have departed, and things do not look hopeful. It seems that the same awful heat which caused your own collapse has left your cats ill-tempered and unmanageable. Our visit to the water park was a disaster. Needless to say, we all want the cats to be happy, but I am certain that they would be happier at home. Please contact me privately and I will put them on the next bus to Snort City.

Your Sincere Neighbor,
Ike

P.S. If you act quickly, Mrs. LaRue and I can still make it onto our ship!

July 12, The Empire State Building,
NEW YORK CITY

Dear Mrs. Hibbins,

The view from the observation deck is stunning—unless you're a cat! How was I to know the little scratchers are afraid of heights? When I tried holding them up so that they could get a better view, they turned on me viciously! The security guards completely misread the situation. I was subjected to harsh questioning, which might have ended badly had Mrs. LaRue not arrived to explain.

Your Honest Friend,
Ike

P.S. Hurry, our ship leaves tomorrow!

July 13, BUMBLETUB, OHIO

Dear Mrs. Hibbins,

My ship has sailed, and with it all hopes of a pleasant resolution to this unhappy saga. Traveling instead by car, we have left the coast far behind. I see now why the ship's captain, in his wisdom, refused to accept cats. The creatures simply do not travel well! As we drove through this charming countryside, I became worried about their delicate nerves and suggested that a quiet rest in the cat carrier would do them good. In their manic state they were unable to understand my kindness. I must admit my thoughts stray often to cool ocean breezes and the vacation that might have been.

Wistfully Yours,
Ike

July 14, MINNEBUCKBUCK, MICHIGAN

Dear Mrs. Hibbins,

I thought I spied the ocean today, but Mrs. LaRue said it is merely a "great" lake. I can see nothing great in something so fraudulent. Though we spent the day traveling along this dismal coast, I have not spotted a single cruise ship. My mood sours. I tried to suggest that we have traveled far enough, but Mrs. LaRue stubbornly insists that we must go on. I know that the cats would like to turn back, too, but they are so contrary they refuse to take my side. Only _you_ can end this fiasco!

Beggingly Yours,
Ike

July 15, Big Earl's Motel,
BAZOOKA, WISCONSIN

Dear Mrs. Hibbins,

We were forced to stay in this vile motel, as none of the finer establishments will accept cats. Small wonder! With typical generosity I offered to let them sleep on the wonderful cot Big Earl himself brought in, while I took the hard, lumpy bed for myself. Wouldn't you know, they pitched a fit! The ultimate injustice came when Mrs. LaRue banished _me_ to the car for the night! I went, but only to keep the peace. Please reply quickly—and send bus fare!

Ike

P.S. I slept poorly and now have a stiff neck.

July 16, Dino-Land Theme Park,
PEA GRAVEL, SOUTH DAKOTA

Dear Mrs. Hibbins,

The cats made complete fools of themselves here at "Dino-Land."
They showed no interest in dinosaurs whatsoever, disrupted the
"Jurassic Jungle" ride with their constant meowing, and had to be
asked to leave the gift shop when they overturned the "Catnip
Critters" bin.

Your Embarrassed Neighbor,
Ike

P.S. The local postmaster claims that it would be illegal for me to
send live cats through the mail. I wonder if that could be true.

July 17, Smucky's Diner, BUCKETVILLE, IOWA

Dear Mrs. Hibbins,

I am glad to hear that you are recovering. Things are not so rosy here. For days your cats have been insisting that they will eat only "Bob's" brand gourmet cat food in either the liver or salmon flavors. Yet when we attempted to enjoy a quiet meal at this diner, they accused me of trying to steal their fish platters! Since I know they prefer cat food, I tried to point out the inconsistency of their argument, but with them it's always blame, blame, blame! Now Mrs. LaRue says all our meals must be eaten in the car! Despite my easygoing personality, I wonder how much more I can take!

Unhappily Yours,
Ike

P.S. The fish platters reminded me of the lovely ocean so far away. And cruise ships.

July 18, FLATHEAD, MISSOURI

Dear Mrs. Hibbins,

I have been inventing car games to pass the time. They are invariably clever, but the cats either refuse to play, play badly, or, frankly, <u>cheat</u>! Yesterday we played the "license plate game," in which each player attempts to "collect" plates from different states. Because of my sharp eye and superior knowledge, I always win. Apparently the cats grew frustrated, because when I spotted a truck with Oklahoma plates, <u>they</u> claimed to have seen it first! A terrible argument ensued. Finally Mrs. LaRue pulled over and I was forced to apologize, even though I had done nothing wrong. Since then, despite the heat outside, we have proceeded in chilly silence.

Your Wrongly Accused Neighbor,
Ike

P.S. It isn't really "chilly," that was just my artful way of describing the mood.

July 19, NOSTRIL CREEK, KANSAS

Dear Mrs. Hibbins,

I grow worried about Mrs. LaRue. The strain of this long journey appears to be taking its toll on her. A certain grimness overshadows her usual frolicsome nature. Of course I do all I can to cheer her up, but sometimes even my own high spirits begin to sag. The open prairie drifts by like an endless sea, making me think how much better we would feel (Mrs. LaRue and I) if we were relaxing aboard a mighty ocean liner. Instead, fate has trapped us in this small, hot car with nothing to look at but the dusty plain. And cats. Sigh.

Ike

Dear Mrs. Hibbins,

July 20, MOUNT LULU, COLORADO

The cats have been stealing my chew toys, shedding on my pillows, and clawing my suitcases. Their poor manners have forced me to set limits, so I used masking tape to divide the car's passenger area in half. Now they insist that they should have more than half because there are <u>two</u> of them! They also claim that the radio is on <u>their</u> side! I am forced to listen to this crazy talk all day long, while outside the plains give way to towering peaks. I begin to wonder if this terrible journey will ever end. Perhaps I will mail <u>myself</u> home from the next post office!

Ike

P.S. That was a bitter joke, in case you are wondering.
P.P.S. I'm still worried about Mrs. LaRue.
P.P.P.S. I'm running out of bones!

July 22, THE GRAND CANYON, ARIZONA

Dear Mrs. Hibbins,

Is it really a "Grand" Canyon? In my sad state I can no longer tell. Days of endless travel, poor food, lumpy mattresses, and unpleasant company(!) have left me but a pale shadow of my former self. I almost envy the lowly burros who have carried us into this pit. Compared to me, their lives seem simple and carefree. I am down to my last bone. This cannot go on much longer!

Desperately Yours,
Ike

P.S. I find your failure to respond unsettling.

The Snort City Register/Gazette

July 24

CAR TROUBLE
STALLS VACATION!
LARUES TO CRUISE

DEATH VALLEY, CALIFORNIA. The famous valley claimed another victim yesterday as the car belonging to Snort City's Gertrude LaRue overheated and died. LaRue, her dog, Ike, and two cats belonging to neighbor Leona Hibbins were rescued by a passing motorist. The mechanical failure occurred after a dog bone somehow became lodged inside the car's engine. "We were lucky to be rescued!" said Mrs. LaRue.

Even luckier was the fact that their rescuer turned out to be Gustav Blim, First Mate on the SS *Mermaid*, a cruise ship based in Los Angeles. Taking sympathy on LaRue and her companions, Blim offered them berths on his ship, which departs tomorrow for New York. "He was so kind!" gushed LaRue. "And it's a wonderful ship. Even the cats are welcome."

Snort City

July 30, Aboard the SS Mermaid,
ACAPULCO, MEXICO

Dear Mrs. Hibbins,

I just wanted to let you know that your cats and I are doing well. It seems that the difficulties of our recent travels together have made us friends at last! Mexico is wonderful. Last night we played mariachi music into the wee hours!

Adiós for now,
Ike

P.S. Unfortunately we woke up Mrs. LaRue, who nevertheless is recovering splendidly from her seasickness.